Great Journevs

Content:  D1362890

Great Journeys

Get the facts

The first great journey

The first modern human beings lived in **Africa** about **150 thousand years ago**.

They lived in the part of Africa now known as Sudan, Kenya and Tanzania.

The people started migrating to new places. This may have been because

○ the climate changed

○ there were too many people and they needed more space.

The most amazing journey in human history had begun!

About **100 thousand years ago**, humans settled in **south** and **west Africa**.

About **70 thousand years ago** human beings reached the **Near East**.

They reached **Asia** and **Australia** about **60 thousand years ago**.

Forty thousand years ago they reached **Europe**. Some scientists think they may have travelled by raft.

Less than **30 thousand years ago** people crossed into **North America** from **Asia**.

From there they travelled down to **South America**.

When people reached the **Pacific islands**, the journey was done!

7

Discovering America

Many people *think* **Christopher Columbus** discovered America in **1492**.

But:

- There were already people there.

- Other people from Europe had probably got there first.

Columbus reached many islands. He reached the **coast** of South America. He never reached the **mainland** of North America.

A copy of Columbus' ship 'Santa Maria'

Leif Ericson was probably the **first person from Europe** to reach America.

He was born in **Iceland** around the year **980**.

He reached North America in about the year **1000**.

No one knows exactly where he landed, but it was probably in what is now Newfoundland. He called the country **Vinland** because of the wild grapes (**vines**) growing there.

So who really discovered America?

The people who crossed from Asia thousands of years before and became **Native Americans**.

Native Americans today.

Darwin and the Beagle

The Beagle was the ship that sailed on one of the greatest ever scientific journeys. In 1831 it set out to explore the coast of South America.

The captain of the ship was Robert Fitzroy.

He wanted someone to come with him who could be a friend and who could study wildlife.

Robert Fitzroy

Charles Darwin

He chose Charles Darwin, a young man of 22.

Galapagos Islands

South America

In 1835 The Beagle reached the Galapagos Islands.

Darwin noticed that the birds and animals on each island were slightly different.

Each island had its own type of *finch*. They had changed over thousands of years to suit the food found on that island.

Beak for eating seeds.

Beak for eating insects and fruit.

When he got back to England, Darwin realised how important this was.

It showed how plants and animals develop. He called his ideas the Theory of Natural Selection.

The Northwest Passage

The journey to the Pacific **around South America** is very difficult.

For nearly five hundred years, sailors looked for a route to the north of **North America**.

They called this route the **Northwest Passage**. The problem is that for most of the time the sea is frozen.

In **1845 Sir John Franklin** led an expedition to find the passage. The expedition never came back.

In the winter of 1846 the two ships were trapped in ice. **Franklin died** in **1847**.

In **1848** the survivors tried to escape across the ice by sledge, but no one survived.

The food they took with them may have made them ill. The tins of meat were sealed up with lead.

Lead poisoning makes people weak and confused. In 1981, some bodies were found. They had high levels of lead in their bodies.

The **first person** to sail through the Northwest Passage was **Roald Amundsen**. It took him three years, from 1903 to 1906.

Roald Amundsen

A way for large ships to pass to the north of America wasn't found until 1957.

A much easier way to go from the Atlantic to the Pacific is the **Panama Canal**. This was opened in 1914.

Because of **climate change**, the ice is melting. By 2050 big ships may be able to use the Northwest passage all the year round.

The South Pole

The first people to reach the South Pole were **Roald Amundsen** and his team.

At that time, the only way to reach the South Pole was across the ice.

Amundsen set off in **October 1911**. There were five men, four sledges and fifty-two dogs!

They reached the South Pole on December 14th.

Sixteen of the dogs were still alive. Many had been killed to feed the other dogs.

The trip to the Pole and back took **99 days** and covered **1,860 miles**.

Captain Scott reached the South Pole a month after Amundsen. All of his team died on the return journey.

No one else reached the South Pole until **1956**, when people flew there by **aeroplane**.

There is now a **science base** at the South Pole. People live and work there all the year round.

Apollo 11

On July 20th 1969, the moon lander **Eagle** broke away from the command module **Columbia** in orbit around the Moon and landed on the Moon's surface.

Six hours later, **Neil Armstrong** went outside. He was the **first man** to stand on the Moon.

The astronaut **Buzz Aldrin** came out of the lander and was the **second person** on the Moon.

Neil and Buzz gathered rocks to bring back to Earth.

Twenty one hours later, Eagle took off and met up with the command module, where **Michael Collins** was waiting for them.

This was the first of the Apollo missions that landed on the Moon. There were six other missions.

Apollo 12

Landed 19th November 1969

Carried out experiments. Landed next to the Surveyor 3 spacecraft that had been on the Moon for 2.5 years.

Apollo 13

Launched 11th April 1970

An on-board explosion meant they could not land on the Moon and had to come straight back to Earth.

Apollo 14

Landed 5th February 1971

Commander Alan Shepard played golf on the Moon!

Apollo 15

Landed 30th July 1971

The Lunar Rover was used for the first time.

Apollo 16

Landed 21st April 1972

Visited a mountain region of the Moon for the first time.

Apollo 17

Landed 7th December 1972

Eugene Cernan – the last man on the Moon – so far!

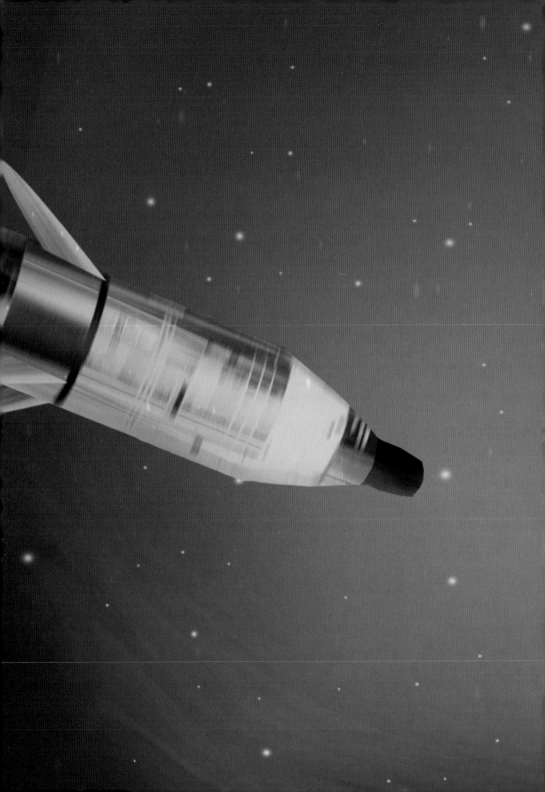

The
Big Sleep

Chapter 1:
The greatest journey ever

Pete Smith had thought about it for months.

He would be famous. He would be going on the greatest journey ever.

He had been training for years to be the first man to go to the stars.

Astronomers had found a star with planets. One of the planets was just like the Earth.

But it would take fifty years to get there.

Pete Smith was training to be an astronaut. He would be the first person to reach the stars ...
But it would take him fifty years to get there!

"We haven't found a way to travel faster than light," the scientists had said.

"But we can put you to sleep. You will sleep for fifty years, and wake up when you get there. You won't get any older."

But everyone else would. It would take a hundred years to get there and back.

Everyone he knew on Earth would be dead.

He would never see Sammie again.

Chapter 2:
"You'll have to forget me"

Sammie was Pete's girlfriend. At first he hadn't told her about the space mission.

But the mission would start soon.

He took Sammie to one of their favourite places.

He told her about the mission.

"It'll be a hundred years before I get back. You'll be long dead. You'll have to forget me, Sammie, and find someone else."

The day of the launch arrived. Pete climbed into his special sleep pod. A special gas was pumped in.

Before he fell asleep, Pete thought about Sammie.

She had tried to make him change his mind. But Pete knew he couldn't. Hundreds of people worked on the mission. He couldn't let them down.

The pod got colder and colder. Pete's body would be frozen – for fifty years!

Chapter 3:
The launch

The pod was loaded into the space ship.

All of Pete's family were there to watch. But Sammie stayed at home. She couldn't bear the thought that she would never see Pete again.

The launch was perfect. Soon, Pete's frozen body was on its way to the stars!

The space ship travelled on through space. It left the solar system far behind. Pete was going faster than anyone had gone before, but he knew nothing about it.

Ahead of him, a star grew slowly bigger. Around this star was the Earth-like planet the astronomers had found.

But what would Pete find there? Would there be life? And would it be friendly?

For years, the space ship travelled through space ...

At last the space ship reached an Earth-like planet. But what would Pete find there?

Chapter 4:
Arrival

At last, Pete's space ship arrived at the planet. Machines on the space ship started to work. Special gas was pumped into the pod. Slowly, Pete's body was warmed up.

He opened his eyes and sat up. It seemed like only yesterday he had gone to sleep.

The ship headed down towards the planet. It was covered in green forest, and looked just like the Earth. But what would he find there?

The airlock door opened and Pete stepped out. He heard a sound overhead.

A helicopter!

The helicopter landed and people got out. And the first person he saw was Sammie!

"It happened just after you left," said Sammie. "They discovered a way to travel faster than light! People have been on this planet for years, waiting for you."

"But what about you?" said Pete. "You should be seventy years old by now!"

Sammie laughed.

"I made them put me to sleep for fifty years too!"

Great Journeys word check

climate

climate change

command module

expedition

experiments

mainland

migration

mission

moon lander

Native Americans

natural selection

North-west passage

scientific

scientist

settled

survivors